I0822555

The Call of Cthulhu

A Mind-Bending Mythos of Cosmic Dread, Ancient Gods & Insanity Beyond the Stars

A Modern Translation

Adapted for the Contemporary Reader

H.P. Lovecraft

Translated by Tim Zengerink

Table of Contents

Preface
Message to the Reader

Rebuilding the Greatest Library in Human History

Thousands of years ago, the Library of Alexandria was the heart of global knowledge — a sanctuary where the wisdom of every known civilization was gathered and shared freely.

And then, it was lost.

Now, we're rebuilding it — and you are invited to join us.

At the Library of Alexandria, we've set out to make every book available to every person on Earth — not just in print, but in every language, every format, and for every reader.

Here's how we do it:

- **Deluxe Print Editions at True Printing Cost** - Order any book as a high-quality paperback, elegant hardcover, or stunning boxset — and only pay what it costs to print. No markups. No middlemen.
- **Unlimited Access to the Greatest Works** - Enjoy thousands of timeless classics — from Plato to Shakespeare to Tolstoy — in beautiful, modern eBook and audiobook editions. Read and listen without limits — for every reader, everywhere.
- **Modern Translations for Every Language & Dialect** - We're reimagining the classics in clear, accessible language — and translating them into every dialect imaginable. Everyone deserves to understand humanity's greatest ideas.

When you visit **LibraryofAlexandria.com**, you're not just accessing books — you're joining a global movement to restore, preserve, and share the wisdom of civilization.

Join us today at LibraryofAlexandria.com

Together, we'll ensure the light of human wisdom never fades again.

With gratitude,

The Modern Library of Alexandria Team

Visit:
www.libraryofalexandria.com
Or scan the code below:

Introduction

The Birth of Cosmic Horror

Few stories in modern literature have reshaped the landscape of horror as profoundly as H.P. Lovecraft's *The Call of Cthulhu*. First published in the February 1928 issue of Weird Tales, this story is not merely a tale of monsters or haunted places, but a revelation of humankind's insignificance in the face of a universe governed by incomprehensible and indifferent cosmic forces. With *The Call of Cthulhu*, Lovecraft effectively crystallized his vision of "cosmic horror," a genre-defining concept that would go on to influence generations of writers, filmmakers, and creators across all mediums.

The narrative of *The Call of Cthulhu* is deceptively straightforward. It unfolds through the fragmented accounts of Francis Wayland Thurston, who pieces together a horrifying truth from various documents, newspaper clippings, and eyewitness testimonies. These disparate sources converge around a singular, terrifying revelation: an ancient, alien entity named Cthulhu—a monstrous being of unimaginable power—once ruled the Earth and now lies dormant beneath the Pacific Ocean in the sunken city of R'lyeh, waiting for the stars to align so it can rise again. Though humanity is largely unaware of its existence, scattered cults and dreamers remain connected to this cosmic entity, sensing its slumbering presence and preparing for the day of its awakening.

At its core, *The Call of Cthulhu* is less about direct confrontation with a monster and more about the unsettling realization of humanity's fragility. Lovecraft's protagonist does not defeat Cthulhu, nor does he even see the creature firsthand. Instead, the story builds its terror through the slow unveiling of forbidden knowledge—knowledge so profound that it challenges the very notion of human understanding. This is a defining hallmark of Lovecraft's work: the idea that true horror lies not in death or violence but in the crushing awareness that our existence is meaningless within a vast, uncaring cosmos.

To appreciate *The Call of Cthulhu*, it is essential to understand the literary and philosophical context in which Lovecraft wrote. Unlike the gothic horror of the 19th century, which often revolved around supernatural elements grounded in human morality—such as vengeful ghosts or cursed families—Lovecraft's horror was rooted in materialist and existential thought. Influenced by writers like Edgar Allan Poe, Lord Dunsany, and Algernon Blackwood, as well as by the scientific discoveries of his time, Lovecraft rejected the notion that the universe was orderly or benevolent. For him, the cosmos was an incomprehensible expanse filled with forces so ancient and alien that they rendered human concerns trivial.

This worldview gave rise to a distinctive form of horror. In *The Call of Cthulhu*, the terror is not simply that Cthulhu exists, but that its existence suggests a universe teeming with entities beyond our comprehension—beings for whom humanity is as insignificant as ants are to us. The story repeatedly emphasizes this point, reminding readers that human history, religion, and civilization are mere flickers against the backdrop of deep time and interstellar reality. Cthulhu is not "evil" in the traditional sense; it simply exists, indifferent to our concepts of morality or survival.

What makes this story particularly powerful is Lovecraft's narrative technique. Rather than presenting events in a linear fashion, he uses a fragmented, investigative structure that mirrors the piecemeal nature of forbidden knowledge. The reader, like Thurston, is drawn deeper into the mystery through second-hand accounts, cryptic dreams, and strange artifacts. This approach creates a sense of authenticity—as if the story is not fiction, but a disturbing record of real events that have been deliberately obscured from public awareness. Lovecraft's mastery of tone, his blending of scholarly language with moments of vivid, hallucinatory description, heightens the story's sense of unease.

Yet beyond its literary merits, *The Call of Cthulhu* represents a turning point in the evolution of horror fiction. It moves away from the personal fears of gothic literature—fear of death, sin, or madness—and toward a fear of the unknown on a cosmic scale. In doing so, Lovecraft laid the foundation for what we now call the "Cthulhu Mythos," a sprawling fictional universe that would expand through his own stories and those of other writers inspired by his vision. The mythos encompasses not only Cthulhu but a pantheon of ancient beings—Nyarlathotep, Yog-Sothoth, Azathoth—each embodying aspects of the incomprehensible cosmos.

For readers approaching *The Call of Cthulhu* for the first time, this introduction serves as a guide to navigating its themes, symbolism, and cultural impact. To fully appreciate Lovecraft's work, one must look beyond the surface narrative of cultists and sea monsters and engage with the deeper philosophical questions it raises. What does it mean to live in a universe where human beings are not the center of creation? How do we confront the terror of the unknown without succumbing to despair? And how can a story written nearly a century ago still resonate so powerfully with modern readers?

Themes of Insanity, Forbidden Knowledge, and Cosmic Dread

One of the most striking elements of *The Call of Cthulhu* is its exploration of insanity—not as a personal failing but as a natural response to the incomprehensible. Throughout the story, characters who come into direct contact with Cthulhu or its influence often descend into madness. Sculptors are plagued by visions, sailors lose their sanity upon encountering the creature's cult, and dreamers are driven to hysteria by glimpses of a reality that should not exist. Lovecraft suggests that the human mind, bound by the limitations of perception and reason, cannot endure the full truth of the universe. Knowledge, in this context, is both power and poison.

This theme of forbidden knowledge is central to Lovecraft's philosophy. In his essay "Supernatural Horror in Literature," Lovecraft argued that the greatest fear is fear of the unknown. *The Call of Cthulhu* embodies this principle by slowly revealing fragments of a larger, more terrifying truth—just enough to unsettle but never enough to fully explain. The titular creature, though described in some detail, remains largely beyond comprehension. Its alien biology and motives are not fully explicable, and this ambiguity makes it even more terrifying. Unlike traditional monsters, which can often be defeated or understood, Cthulhu represents something eternal and beyond human grasp.

Lovecraft also uses the motif of dreams as a gateway to the cosmic unknown. Several characters in the story experience vivid and disturbing dreams connected to Cthulhu's presence. These dreams serve as both warnings and transmissions, suggesting that the barrier between our world and the realm of the Great Old Ones is thinner than we realize. The subconscious mind, unbound by rational thought, becomes a conduit for truths too immense for waking consciousness.

The story's structure further enhances its sense of inevitability and dread. By the time Thurston uncovers the full scope of the Cthulhu cult and its history, the reader realizes that humanity's fate is precarious at best. Cthulhu may be dormant, but its eventual awakening feels inevitable—a matter not of if, but when. Lovecraft leaves us with the chilling understanding that even if we remain blissfully ignorant of these cosmic forces, they remain indifferent to us, biding their time.

This philosophical undercurrent—often referred to as "cosmicism"—is perhaps Lovecraft's most enduring contribution to horror. Unlike traditional narratives where humans are active agents battling evil, Lovecraftian horror places us as passive observers in a universe far beyond our control. Our victories are temporary, our knowledge incomplete, and our significance negligible. This worldview can be unsettling, even nihilistic, but it is also oddly liberating. By recognizing our smallness, we may come to appreciate the grandeur and mystery of existence without the need for comforting illusions.

The Legacy of Lovecraft and the Cthulhu Mythos

The influence of *The Call of Cthulhu* cannot be overstated. It is the cornerstone of the Cthulhu Mythos, a fictional universe that has grown far beyond Lovecraft's original stories. Writers such as August Derleth, Robert E. Howard, Ramsey Campbell, and Brian Lumley have expanded on Lovecraft's ideas, creating new deities, settings, and tales that interweave with his original vision. Beyond literature, the mythos has permeated popular culture through films, tabletop games like Call of Cthulhu, video games, comic books, and music. The iconic image of Cthulhu—a tentacled, dragon-like entity slumbering beneath the waves—has become a symbol not only of horror but of the fascination with the unknown.

Yet Lovecraft's impact is not solely due to his imaginative world-building. His unique narrative voice, blending meticulous realism with surreal, nightmarish imagery, set a new standard for horror writing. His stories read like found documents or scholarly investigations, blurring the line between fiction and reality. This "pseudo-documentary" style lends his tales a sense of authenticity that makes their horrors all the more convincing.

At the same time, Lovecraft's work is not without controversy. His personal views—particularly his xenophobia and racism—have been widely criticized, and modern readers often struggle to reconcile the brilliance of his cosmic vision with the prejudice reflected in some of his writings. While *The Call of Cthulhu* itself is less overtly problematic in this regard, it is important to approach Lovecraft with a critical eye, acknowledging both his contributions and his flaws. In many ways, the ongoing adaptation and reinvention of the Cthulhu Mythos by contemporary authors—many of whom seek to diversify and subvert Lovecraft's original narratives—demonstrates the resilience and adaptability of his ideas.

For readers today, *The Call of Cthulhu* remains a compelling and unsettling experience. It is not a story of resolution or comfort; it does not offer heroes who triumph or villains who are vanquished. Instead, it offers a glimpse into a reality that is fundamentally alien, where the very act of knowing becomes dangerous. This makes it both timeless and uniquely modern, resonating in an age where we continue to grapple with forces—technological, environmental, cosmic—that are beyond our complete understanding.

As you embark on your journey into *The Call of Cthulhu*, prepare to encounter not just a story, but an idea—a vision of the universe that is at once terrifying and awe-inspiring. Allow yourself to be drawn into its atmosphere of dread, its carefully constructed mystery, and its profound philosophical implications. And remember: in the world of Lovecraft, the greatest horrors are not always those we can see, but those we can only imagine.

The Call of Cthulhu

> "There may conceivably be a survival of such great powers or beings ... a survival from an enormously distant time when ... consciousness was perhaps expressed in shapes and forms that have long since retreated before the advancing wave of humanity ... forms that only poetry and legend have managed to capture in fleeting memories and have named gods, monsters, and mythical creatures of every type and variety...."
>
> —Algernon Blackwood.

> "The circle of worshipers moved in endless revelry between the circle of bodies and the circle of fire."

The Horror in Clay.

I believe the greatest mercy in the world is that the human mind cannot connect all of its knowledge together. We exist on a calm island of ignorance surrounded by endless black oceans of the unknown, and we were never supposed to travel very far from it. The various sciences, each pursuing their own paths, have caused us little harm so far; but someday when we start putting together all these separate pieces of knowledge, it will reveal such horrifying views of reality and our terrible place within it that we will either lose our sanity from what we discover or run away from this devastating truth back into the safety and peace of a new age of darkness.

Theosophists have speculated about the magnificent scale of the cosmic cycle in which our world and humanity represent brief moments. They have suggested mysterious survivals using language that would terrify us if it weren't softened by cheerful optimism. However, it wasn't from them that I received the single vision of forbidden ages that chills me when I consider it and drives me to madness when I dream about it. That vision, like all terrifying glimpses of reality, emerged from an accidental connection of unrelated elements—in this instance, an old newspaper article and the research notes of a deceased professor. I pray that no one else will make this same connection; certainly, if I remain alive, I will never deliberately provide a piece to such a horrifying puzzle. I believe that the professor also planned to remain silent about what he had discovered, and that he would have destroyed his notes if sudden death hadn't claimed him.

My understanding of this matter started during the winter of 1926-27 when my great-uncle died—George Gammell Angell, Professor Emeritus of Semitic languages at Brown University in Providence, Rhode Island. Professor Angell was well-known as an expert on ancient inscriptions and was frequently consulted by directors of major museums, so his death at ninety-two was remembered by many people. In the local area, interest grew because of the mysterious circumstances surrounding his death. The professor had collapsed while walking home from the Newport boat, suddenly falling down, according to witnesses, after being bumped into by a sailor-looking Black man who had emerged from one of the strange dark alleyways on the steep hillside that served as a shortcut from the waterfront to the deceased's house on Williams Street. Doctors couldn't find any obvious medical problem, but after confused discussion they decided that some hidden heart condition, brought on by an elderly man climbing such a steep hill so quickly, had caused his death. At that time I had no reason to disagree with this conclusion, but lately I find myself questioning it—and doing much more than just questioning.

As my great-uncle's heir and executor, since he died as a childless widower, I was expected to thoroughly examine his papers; for this purpose, I moved his complete collection of files and boxes to my apartment in Boston. Much of the material I organized will later be published by the American Archaeological Society, but there was one box that I found extremely puzzling and felt very reluctant to show to anyone else. It had been locked, and I didn't find the key until it occurred to me to examine the personal ring that the professor always carried in his pocket. Then I was able to open it, but when I did, I seemed only to face an even greater and more tightly sealed mystery. What could possibly be the meaning of the strange clay bas-relief and the disconnected notes, wandering thoughts, and clippings that I discovered? Had my uncle, in his final years, become gullible to the most shallow frauds? I decided to track down the unusual sculptor responsible for this apparent disruption of an elderly man's peace of mind.

The bas-relief formed a crude rectangle, less than an inch thick and roughly five by six inches in size, clearly made in recent times. Yet its designs carried an atmosphere and meaning that felt anything but modern. While cubism and futurism embrace many strange and bold expressions, they rarely capture that mysterious, systematic quality found in ancient writing. Most of these designs appeared to be some form of writing, though despite my extensive knowledge of my uncle's papers and collections, I couldn't identify this specific type or even guess at its distant origins.

Above these mysterious symbols was a figure that was clearly meant to be a picture, though its rough, impressionistic style made it difficult to understand exactly what it depicted. It appeared to be some kind of monster, or a symbol meant to represent a monster, with a shape that only a sick mind could have imagined. If I describe it as triggering images in my overactive imagination of an octopus, a dragon, and a distorted human figure all at once, I would be capturing the essence of what I saw. A soft, tentacled head sat atop a bizarre and scaly body that had underdeveloped wings; but it was the overall shape of the entire creature that made it so terrifyingly awful. Behind the figure, there was a faint outline of what looked like massive, ancient architecture.

The documents that came with this strange item were written in Professor Angell's most recent handwriting, along with a pile of newspaper clippings, and didn't attempt any fancy literary style. The main document appeared to be titled "CTHULHU CULT" in carefully printed letters to prevent anyone from misreading such an unfamiliar word. This manuscript was split into two parts: the first section was titled "1925—Dream and Dream Work of H. A. Wilcox, 7 Thomas St., Providence, R. I.," and the second was labeled "Narrative of Inspector John R. Legrasse, 121 Bienville St., New Orleans, La., at 1908 A. A. S. Mtg—Notes on Same, & Prof. Webb's Acct." The remaining manuscript pages consisted entirely of short notes, including some accounts describing the strange dreams of various individuals, some references from mystical books and publications (particularly W. Scott-Eliott's Atlantis and the Lost Lemuria), and additional commentary on long-lasting secret societies and hidden cults, with citations from mythological and anthropological reference works like Frazer's Golden Bough and Miss Murray's Witch-Cult in Western Europe. The newspaper clippings mostly referred to bizarre mental disorders and episodes of collective madness or hysteria during the spring of 1925.

The first half of the main manuscript told a very strange story. It seems that on March 1st, 1925, a thin, dark young man with a nervous and agitated appearance had visited Professor Angell, bringing with him an unusual clay bas-relief that was extremely wet and freshly made. His business card showed the name Henry Anthony Wilcox, and my uncle had recognized him as the youngest son of a respectable family he knew slightly, who had recently been studying sculpture at the Rhode Island School of Design and living by himself at the Fleur-de-Lys Building near that school. Wilcox was a gifted young man of recognized talent but considerable oddness, and had since childhood drawn attention through the bizarre tales and strange dreams he regularly shared. He described himself as "psychically hypersensitive," but the conservative residents of the old commercial city simply considered him "weird." Never socializing much with others his age, he had slowly faded from public view, and was now known only to a small circle of art enthusiasts from other cities. Even the Providence Art Club, eager to maintain its traditional values, had found him completely impossible.

During the visit, according to the professor's manuscript, the sculptor suddenly asked his host to use his archaeological expertise to help identify the hieroglyphics carved on the bas-relief. He spoke in a distant, artificial way that seemed pretentious and made it hard to feel any connection with him; my uncle responded with some irritation, since the obviously fresh appearance of the tablet suggested it had nothing to do with real archaeology. Young

Wilcox's response, which made such an impression on my uncle that he remembered and wrote down every word, had an incredibly poetic quality that must have been typical of how he always spoke, and which I've since learned is very much his style. He said, "It is new, indeed, for I made it last night in a dream of strange cities; and dreams are older than brooding Tyre, or the contemplative Sphinx, or garden-girdled Babylon."

It was at that moment he started telling his wandering story, which suddenly stirred a dormant memory and captured my uncle's intense attention. There had been a minor earthquake the previous night, the most significant one felt in New England in several years, and Wilcox's imagination had been deeply affected by it. When he went to bed, he experienced an extraordinary dream of massive Cyclopean cities built from enormous blocks and towering monoliths that stretched toward the sky, all covered in green slime and filled with an ominous, hidden terror. Ancient symbols decorated the walls and columns, and from somewhere deep below came a voice that wasn't really a voice at all—a confused sensation that only imagination could transform into sound, which he tried to express through an almost impossible combination of letters: "Cthulhu fhtagn".

This confusing mix of words was what triggered the memory that both excited and troubled Professor Angell. He questioned the sculptor with scientific precision and examined with nearly frantic focus the carved relief that the young man had found himself working on while dressed only in his nightclothes, awakening in complete bewilderment. My uncle later blamed his advanced age, Wilcox said, for being slow to recognize both the hieroglyphic symbols and the pictorial design. Many of his questions seemed completely inappropriate to his visitor, particularly those that attempted to link him with strange cults or secret societies; and Wilcox couldn't comprehend the repeated offers of secrecy he received in return for admitting membership in some widespread mystical or pagan religious organization. When Professor Angell became certain that the sculptor truly knew nothing about any cult or system of hidden knowledge, he bombarded his visitor with requests for future dream reports. This approach proved successful, as after that first meeting the manuscript documents daily visits from the young man, during which he described disturbing pieces of nighttime visions that always centered on some horrifying massive vista of dark and wet stone, accompanied by an underground voice or presence chanting monotonously in mysterious sensory impressions that could only be described as nonsense. The two sounds most often repeated are those represented by the letters "Cthulhu" and "R'lyeh".

On March 23rd, the manuscript went on, Wilcox didn't show up; and when people checked his apartment, they discovered he had come down with some kind of mysterious fever and been taken to his family's home on Waterman Street. He had screamed during the night, waking up several other artists in the building, and since then had only shown periods of being unconscious mixed with episodes of delirium. My uncle immediately called the family, and from that point on kept a close eye on the situation; frequently visiting the Thayer Street office of Dr. Tobey, who he found out was handling the case. The young man's feverish mind seemed to be focused on bizarre things; and the doctor would shudder from time to time when he talked about them. These visions included not just a repeat of what he had previously dreamed, but also wild references to a massive thing "miles high" that walked or moved clumsily around. He never completely described this creature, but scattered frantic words, as Dr. Tobey repeated them, convinced the professor that it had to be the same as the unnamed monster he had tried to create in his dream-sculpture. Any mention of this creature, the doctor noted, always led to the young man falling back into a state of lethargy. His temperature, strangely enough, wasn't much higher than normal; but everything else about his condition suggested genuine fever rather than a mental illness.

On April 2nd at around 3 p.m., every sign of Wilcox's illness suddenly disappeared. He sat up straight in bed, shocked to discover himself at home and completely unaware of what had occurred in dreams or reality since the night of March 22nd. Declared healthy by his doctor, he went back to his lodgings three days later; however, he could provide no additional help to Professor Angell. All evidence of his strange dreams had disappeared along with his recovery, and my uncle stopped recording his nighttime thoughts after a week of meaningless and unrelated descriptions of completely ordinary visions.

Here the first part of the manuscript ended, but references to certain scattered notes gave me a great deal to think about—so much, in fact, that only the deep-rooted skepticism that was then shaping my worldview can explain why I continued to distrust the artist. The notes I'm referring to were those that described the dreams of various people during the same time period when young Wilcox had experienced his strange visions. My uncle, it appears, had quickly set up an incredibly extensive network of inquiries among nearly all the friends he could question without being rude, asking them to report their nightly dreams and the dates of any remarkable visions they'd had recently. The response to his request seems to have been mixed; but he must have received far more replies than any ordinary person could have managed without help from a secretary. This original correspondence wasn't kept, but his notes formed a comprehensive and truly meaningful summary. Ordinary people in society and business—New England's traditional "salt of the earth"—produced almost entirely negative results, though scattered instances of disturbing but shapeless nighttime impressions appeared here and there, always occurring between March 23rd and April 2nd—the same period as young Wilcox's delirium. Scientists were hardly more affected, though four cases with vague descriptions suggested fleeting glimpses of strange landscapes, and in one case there was mention of a fear of something unnatural.

The answers that mattered came from artists and poets, and I'm certain that panic would have erupted if they had been able to share their experiences with each other. Since I didn't have access to their original letters, I began to suspect that whoever compiled them might have asked suggestive questions or edited the correspondence to support conclusions they had already decided to reach. This is why I kept feeling that Wilcox, who somehow knew about the old information my uncle had collected, was deceiving the experienced scientist. The responses from these creative individuals told a deeply troubling story. Between February 28th and April 2nd, a significant number of them experienced extremely strange dreams, with the dreams becoming far more intense during the time when the sculptor was delirious. More than a quarter of those who reported anything described scenes and partial sounds that were remarkably similar to what Wilcox had described; several dreamers admitted to feeling intense fear of the enormous, unnamed thing that appeared near the end of their dreams. One particular case, which the notes describe with special emphasis, was truly tragic. The person involved, a well-known architect who was interested in theosophy and the occult, became violently insane on the same date as young Wilcox's seizure and died several months later after continuously screaming to be saved from some escaped creature from hell. If my uncle had identified these cases by name rather than just by number, I would have tried to verify them and conduct my own investigation; however, as things stood, I only managed to track down a few of them. All of these cases, though, completely confirmed what the notes said. I've often wondered whether all the people the professor questioned felt as confused as this small group did. It's probably for the best that they will never receive an explanation.

The newspaper clippings, as I've mentioned, covered cases of panic, madness, and strange behavior during that specific time period. Professor Angell must have used a clipping service, because the number of excerpts was enormous, and they came from sources all around the world. There was a nighttime suicide in London, where a solitary sleeper had jumped from a window after letting out a terrifying scream. There was also a rambling letter to the editor of a newspaper in South America, where a fanatic predicted a terrible future based on visions he had experienced. A report from California described a theosophist colony putting on white robes all together for some "glorious fulfillment" that never came, while articles from India spoke cautiously of serious native unrest toward the end of March. Voodoo rituals increased in Haiti, and

African outposts reported threatening murmurs. American officers in the Philippines found certain tribes troublesome around this time, and New York police were attacked by hysterical Levantines on the night of March 22-23. The west of Ireland was also filled with wild rumors and folklore, and a bizarre painter named Ardois-Bonnot displayed a blasphemous Dream Landscape in the Paris spring salon of 1926. The recorded disturbances in mental institutions were so numerous that only a miracle could have prevented the medical community from noticing strange similarities and reaching puzzled conclusions. It was a strange collection of clippings, all things considered; and I can hardly imagine now the cold rationalism with which I dismissed them at the time. But back then I was convinced that young Wilcox had known about the earlier matters the professor had mentioned.

The Tale of Inspector Legrasse.

The earlier events that had made the sculptor's dream and carved relief so meaningful to my uncle formed the focus of the second half of his lengthy manuscript. It seems that Professor Angell had encountered the demonic outlines of the unnamed horror once before, studied the mysterious hieroglyphics, and heard the threatening syllables that can only be written as "Cthulhu"; and all of this occurred in such a disturbing and terrifying context that it's hardly surprising he bombarded young Wilcox with questions and requests for information.

This earlier experience had occurred in 1908, seventeen years before, when the American Archaeological Society held its annual meeting in St. Louis. Professor Angell, as was appropriate for someone of his authority and accomplishments, had played a prominent role in all the discussions; and was among the first to be contacted by the various outsiders who took advantage of the gathering to present questions for accurate answers and problems for expert solutions.

The leader of these visitors, who quickly became the center of attention for the whole gathering, was an ordinary-looking middle-aged man who had journeyed all the way from New Orleans seeking specific information that couldn't be found anywhere locally. His name was John Raymond Legrasse, and he worked as a police inspector. He had brought with him the reason for his visit: a bizarre, disturbing, and seemingly very old stone figurine whose origins he couldn't figure out.

It shouldn't be assumed that Inspector Legrasse had any interest whatsoever in archeology. In fact, his desire for knowledge was driven entirely by professional reasons. The figurine, idol, charm, or whatever it might have been, had been seized several months earlier in the forested marshlands south of New Orleans during a police raid on what was believed to be a voodoo gathering; and the ceremonies associated with it were so strange and horrifying that the police couldn't help but recognize they had discovered a mysterious cult completely unknown to them, and far more evil than even the darkest of the African voodoo groups. Regarding its origins, aside from the wild and incredible stories forced out of the arrested members, absolutely nothing could be learned; this explained why the police were so eager for any historical knowledge that might help them identify the terrifying symbol, and through it trace the cult back to its source.

Inspector Legrasse wasn't ready for the reaction his discovery would cause. Just one look at the object was enough to send the gathered scientists into an intense frenzy of excitement, and they immediately crowded around him to examine the small figure whose complete strangeness and atmosphere of truly ancient origins suggested so powerfully the existence of unexplored and prehistoric realms. No known tradition of sculpture had created this frightening object, yet hundreds and even thousands of years appeared to be etched into its dark and greenish surface made of unidentifiable stone.

The figure, which was eventually passed slowly from person to person for close and careful examination, stood between seven and eight inches tall and displayed exquisitely artistic craftsmanship. It depicted a monster with a vaguely human-like outline, but featured an octopus-like head whose face consisted of a mass of tentacles, a scaly, rubber-like body, enormous claws on both its hind and front feet, and long, narrow wings extending from its back. This creature, which seemed filled with a terrifying and unnatural evil, had a somewhat swollen, corpulent appearance and crouched menacingly on a rectangular block or pedestal covered with indecipherable symbols. The wing tips touched the back edge of the block, the creature's body occupied the center, while the long, curved claws of its folded, crouching hind legs gripped the front edge and extended a quarter of the way down toward the bottom of the pedestal. The tentacled head was bent forward, so that the ends of the facial tentacles brushed against the backs of massive front paws which grasped the crouching figure's raised knees. The appearance of the entire piece was unnaturally lifelike, and all the more subtly frightening because its origin was completely unknown. Its immense, awe-inspiring, and incalculable age was unmistakable; yet it showed no connection whatsoever with any known type of art belonging to civilization's early period—or indeed to any other era.

Completely isolated and distinct, the very substance it was made from remained an enigma; the slippery, dark greenish-black stone with its golden or shimmering specks and bands looked like nothing known to geological or mineralogical science. The symbols carved along the bottom were just as puzzling; and none of the members in attendance, despite representing half the world's specialized knowledge in this area, could develop even the slightest idea of their most distant linguistic connections. These markings, like the object itself and its material, belonged to something terrifyingly ancient and separate from humanity as we understand it; something that disturbingly hinted at old and forbidden cycles of existence in which our world and our understanding have no place.

And yet, as each member shook their head and admitted they couldn't solve the inspector's puzzle, there was one person in that group who sensed something strangely familiar about the grotesque form and script, and who eventually shared with some hesitation the peculiar detail he was aware of. This individual was the late William Channing Webb, professor of anthropology at Princeton University, and an explorer of considerable reputation.

Professor Webb had been involved, forty-eight years earlier, in an expedition to Greenland and Iceland searching for Runic inscriptions that he never managed to discover; and while traveling high up along the West Greenland coast, he had come across an unusual tribe or cult of deteriorated Eskimos whose religion, a strange form of devil-worship, disturbed him with its intentional brutality and disgusting nature. This was a belief system that other Eskimos understood very little about, and which they spoke of only with fear, claiming that it had been passed down from terrifyingly ancient ages before the world was even created. Along with unspeakable ceremonies and human sacrifices, there were specific strange inherited rituals directed toward a supreme elder devil or tornasuk; and Professor Webb had made a detailed phonetic recording from an elderly angekok or wizard-priest, representing the sounds in Roman letters as accurately as he could manage. But what was most important right now was the fetish that this cult had treasured, and around which they performed their dances when the aurora blazed high above the ice cliffs. It was, the professor explained, a very primitive bas-relief made of stone, featuring a horrifying image and some mysterious writing. And as far as he could determine, it was a crude equivalent in all key aspects of the monstrous object now resting before the meeting.

These findings, received with tension and amazement by the gathered members, proved doubly thrilling to Inspector Legrasse; and he immediately began to question his source extensively. Having recorded and transcribed a spoken ritual among the swamp cult-worshipers his officers had captured, he urged the professor to recall as clearly as possible the syllables documented among the devil-worshiping Eskimos. What followed was a thorough comparison of details, and a moment of genuine reverent silence when both the detective and scientist acknowledged the essential similarity of the phrase shared by two demonic rituals separated by such vast distances. What, in essence, both the Eskimo sorcerers and the Louisiana swamp-priests had recited to their related idols was something very much like this—the word-divisions being estimated from customary pauses in the phrase as spoken aloud:

"Ph'nglui mglw'nafh Cthulhu R'lyeh wgah'nagl fhtagn."

Legrasse had an advantage over Professor Webb because some of his mixed-race prisoners had shared with him what the older worshippers had explained the words meant. The text, as it was provided, went something like this:

"In his house at R'lyeh dead Cthulhu waits dreaming."

And now, responding to widespread urgent requests, Inspector Legrasse shared his encounter with the swamp worshipers in complete detail, recounting a story that I could tell held deep meaning for my uncle. The tale had the flavor of the most fantastical visions conceived by creators of myths and spiritual philosophers, and it revealed a remarkable level of cosmic creativity among these mixed-race outcasts who would be the last people anyone would expect to have such imagination.

On November 1st, 1907, New Orleans police received an urgent call for help from the swamp and bayou region to the south. The settlers living there, mostly simple but friendly descendants of Lafitte's crew, were gripped by absolute terror from some unknown force that had crept up on them during the night. It appeared to be voodoo, but a far more horrifying kind than anything they had ever experienced; some of their women and children had vanished since the evil drumbeat had started its relentless pounding deep within the dark, haunted forest where no resident dared to go. There were crazed yelling and bone-chilling screams, spine-tingling chants and dancing demonic fires; and, the terrified messenger explained, the people couldn't endure it any longer.

A group of twenty police officers, traveling in two carriages and one automobile, had departed in the late afternoon with the trembling squatter serving as their guide. When they reached the end of the road that vehicles could travel, they got out and walked for miles in silence through the dreadful cypress swamps where sunlight never penetrated. Twisted roots and sinister hanging strands of Spanish moss surrounded them, and occasionally a heap of wet stones or pieces of a crumbling wall made the oppressive atmosphere even worse with its suggestion of unhealthy human presence—an atmosphere that every deformed tree and every moss-covered patch of land helped to create. Finally, the squatter settlement came into view—a wretched cluster of shacks—and panicked residents rushed out to gather around the group of swaying lanterns. The muted sound of tom-toms could now be heard faintly in the far distance, and a blood-curdling scream echoed at irregular intervals when the wind changed direction. A reddish glow also appeared to seep through the pale vegetation beyond the endless corridors of forest darkness. Too frightened to be left alone again, each of the intimidated squatters absolutely refused to move even one step closer toward the location of the unholy ritual, so Inspector Legrasse and his nineteen fellow officers continued forward without a guide into the dark passages of terror that none of them had ever entered before.

The area the police had now entered was known for its sinister reputation, largely unexplored and untraveled by white people. Stories circulated about a concealed lake that no living person had ever seen, where an enormous, shapeless white creature with glowing eyes was said to live. Local settlers whispered tales of winged demons that emerged from underground caves to pay homage to this being when midnight struck. According to these accounts, the creature had existed there before D'Iberville arrived, before La Salle came, before the Native Americans settled there, and even before the natural wildlife inhabited the forests. It represented pure nightmare, and anyone who laid eyes on it would perish. Yet it influenced people's dreams, which taught them to stay far away from the place. The current voodoo ceremony was actually taking place only at the very edge of this dreaded territory, but even that location was frightening enough; this might explain why the actual site of the ritual had scared the settlers even more than the disturbing sounds and events they witnessed.

Only poetry or madness could capture the sounds that Legrasse's men heard as they pushed forward through the dark swamp toward the red glow and the muted drumbeats. There are vocal sounds that belong to humans, and vocal sounds that belong to animals; and it's horrifying to hear one when you expect the other. Wild animal rage and frenzied abandon reached demonic levels through howls and shrieking fits of ecstasy that ripped through and echoed in those dark woods like plague-bearing storms from the depths of hell. Every so often the chaotic wailing would stop, and from what sounded like a well-trained chorus of rough voices would come a rhythmic chant of that terrible phrase or ceremony:

"Ph'nglui mglw'nafh Cthulhu R'lyeh wgah'nagl fhtagn."

Then the men, after reaching an area where the trees grew more sparsely, suddenly came upon the spectacle itself. Four of them staggered backward, one collapsed unconscious, and two burst into terrified screams that were mercifully drowned out by the wild, chaotic noise of the ritual. Legrasse splashed swamp water onto the unconscious man's face, and they all stood there shaking, almost paralyzed with terror.

In a natural clearing within the swamp sat a grassy island covering roughly an acre, free of trees and reasonably dry. On this space now leaped and contorted a more unimaginable crowd of human deformity than only a Sime or an Angarola could depict. Without clothing, these hybrid creatures were howling, roaring and writhing around a massive ring-shaped bonfire; at the center of which, visible through occasional gaps in the wall of flame, rose a large granite monolith approximately eight feet tall; on top of which, strangely small in comparison, sat the vile carved figurine. From a broad circle of ten scaffolds erected at even intervals with the flame-surrounded monolith at the center dangled, hanging upside down, the strangely mutilated bodies of the defenseless settlers who had vanished. It was within this circle that the ring of worshipers danced and screamed, the overall direction of the group movement flowing from left to right in perpetual revelry between the ring of corpses and the ring of fire.

It might have been just imagination, or perhaps only echoes, that led one of the men—an easily excited Spaniard—to believe he heard responsive chants answering the ritual from some distant and dark place deeper in the woods of ancient legend and terror. I later encountered and interviewed this man, Joseph D. Galvez, and found him to be remarkably imaginative. He even went as far as to suggest he heard the faint sound of enormous wings beating, and claimed to have caught sight of glowing eyes and a massive white form beyond the farthest trees—though I assume he had been listening to too much local folklore.

The men's horrified pause lasted only a short time. Duty took priority, and even though nearly a hundred mixed-race worshipers filled the crowd, the police trusted their weapons and charged resolutely into the disgusting chaos. For five minutes, the resulting noise and disorder defied description. Frenzied strikes were delivered, gunshots rang out, and people fled the scene; but eventually Legrasse managed to count roughly forty-seven sullen captives, forcing them to quickly get dressed and form a line between two rows of officers. Five worshipers had been killed, and two seriously injured ones were transported on makeshift stretchers by their fellow prisoners. The carved figure from the stone monument was naturally handled with care and brought back by Legrasse.

When examined at headquarters following a journey marked by severe stress and exhaustion, the prisoners all turned out to be individuals of very low social standing, mixed racial heritage, and mentally unstable characteristics. The majority were sailors, with a mixture of Black individuals and people of mixed race, primarily West Indians or Brava Portuguese from the Cape Verde Islands, which added elements of voodoo practices to this diverse religious group. However, before many inquiries could be made, it became clear that something much more profound and ancient than African folk magic was at work. Despite being degraded and uneducated, these individuals maintained a remarkably consistent devotion to the core beliefs of their repulsive religion.

They worshipped, according to their claims, the Great Old Ones who existed countless ages before humanity appeared, and who descended to the young world from the heavens. Those Old Ones had vanished now, dwelling within the earth and beneath the ocean; however, their lifeless forms had revealed their mysteries through dreams to the first human, who established a cult that had never perished. This was that very cult, and the captives declared it had always been present and would always continue to exist, concealed in remote wastelands and shadowy locations across the globe until the moment when the great priest Cthulhu, from his dark dwelling in the vast city of R'lyeh beneath the waves, would emerge and once again bring the earth under his dominion. Someday he would summon them, when the stars aligned properly, and the secret cult would forever remain ready to set him free.

Meanwhile, nothing more could be revealed. There existed a secret that even torture was unable to force out. Humanity was not completely alone among the thinking beings of earth, as forms emerged from the darkness to visit the devoted few. However, these were not the Great Old Ones. No person had ever laid eyes on the Old Ones. The carved idol represented great Cthulhu, but no one could determine whether the others resembled him exactly. Nobody could decipher the ancient writing anymore, but knowledge was passed down through spoken words. The sung ritual was not the secret—that was never uttered out loud, only murmured quietly. The chant conveyed only this: "In his house at R'lyeh dead Cthulhu waits dreaming."

Only two of the prisoners were deemed mentally stable enough to face execution by hanging, while the others were sent to different mental institutions. All of them denied taking part in the ritual killings and insisted that the murders had been carried out by Black-winged Ones that had visited them from their ancient gathering place in the cursed forest. However, no clear or consistent explanation about these mysterious allies could ever be obtained. The information that police managed to gather came primarily from an extremely elderly mestizo man named Castro, who claimed he had traveled to exotic ports and spoken with immortal leaders of the cult in the mountains of China.

Old Castro recalled fragments of terrifying legends that made the theories of theosophists seem pale by comparison and rendered humanity and our world appear truly recent and fleeting. There had been countless ages when other Beings dominated the earth, and These entities had possessed magnificent cities. The remnants of These creatures, he explained that the immortal Chinese had informed him, could still be discovered as massive stones on Pacific islands. All of These beings had perished during immense periods of time before humanity emerged, but certain practices existed that could bring Them back to life when the stars had returned to their proper positions in the eternal cycle. These entities had actually originated from the stars themselves, and had carried Their statues along with Them.

These Great Old Ones, Castro went on, weren't made entirely of flesh and blood. They had a physical form—didn't this star-shaped image prove that?—but their form wasn't constructed from ordinary matter. When the stars aligned properly, They could travel from one world to another across the heavens; but when the stars were in the wrong position, They couldn't survive. Yet even though They no longer lived, They would never truly perish. They all rested in stone dwellings within Their magnificent city of R'lyeh, kept intact by the powerful spells of mighty Cthulhu for a magnificent return to life when the stars and the earth would once again be prepared for Them. However, when that moment arrived, some external force would need to help free Their physical forms. The same spells that kept Them perfectly preserved also stopped Them from taking any first action, and They could only remain conscious in the darkness and contemplate while countless millions of years passed. They understood everything happening throughout the universe, since Their way of communicating was through transmitted thoughts. Even at this moment They conversed within Their burial chambers. When, after endless ages of disorder, the first humans appeared, the Great Old Ones reached out to those who were receptive by shaping their dreams; this was the only way Their language could connect with the physical minds of mammals.

Then Castro whispered that those early humans created the cult around small statues that the Great Ones had revealed to them—statues brought from distant stars in ancient times. This cult would persist until the stars aligned properly once more, and the hidden priests would remove mighty Cthulhu from His grave to awaken His followers and restore His dominion over the earth. The moment would be unmistakable, for humanity would have transformed into beings like the Great Old Ones—unrestrained and savage, existing beyond concepts of good and evil, having cast aside all laws and moral codes while people everywhere screamed and murdered and celebrated with wild abandon. At that time, the freed Old Ones would show them fresh methods of screaming and murdering and celebrating and finding pleasure, and the entire world would burn with a devastating inferno of rapture and liberation. Until then, the cult must preserve the memory of those primordial practices through proper ceremonies and hint at the prophecy of their eventual return.

In ancient times, chosen individuals had communicated with the buried Old Ones through dreams, but then something occurred. The massive stone city of R'lyeh, with its towering monuments and tombs, had disappeared beneath the ocean; and the deep waters, filled with that fundamental mystery which even thoughts cannot penetrate, had severed the ghostly communication. However, memory never faded, and the high priests declared that the city would emerge again when the stars aligned properly. Then from the earth came the dark spirits of the land, musty and shadowy, carrying vague whispers gathered in caves beneath long-forgotten ocean floors. But old Castro refused to say much about these beings. He stopped himself abruptly, and no amount of convincing or clever questioning could draw out more information on this topic. The size of the Old Ones was also something he strangely refused to discuss. Regarding the cult, he mentioned that he believed its headquarters was located in the trackless deserts of Arabia, where Irem, the City of Pillars, lies dreaming in hidden isolation. It had no connection to the European witch-cult, and remained practically unknown outside its membership. No book had ever truly suggested its existence, though the immortal Chinese claimed that the Necronomicon of the insane Arab Abdul Alhazred contained hidden meanings that the initiated could interpret as they wished, particularly the widely debated couplet:

"That is not dead which can eternal lie,"

"And with strange eons even death may die."

Legrasse felt deeply impressed and quite bewildered as he searched unsuccessfully for information about the cult's historical connections. Castro had apparently been truthful when he claimed the organization was completely secret. The experts at Tulane University couldn't provide any insight into either the cult or the image, and now the detective had approached the nation's top authorities only to encounter nothing more than Professor Webb's Greenland story.

The intense excitement that Legrasse's story generated at the meeting, backed up as it was by the statuette, is reflected in the letters exchanged afterward among those who were present, though little mention appears in the society's official publication. Those who regularly deal with occasional fraud and deception naturally exercise caution first. Legrasse allowed Professor Webb to borrow the image for a while, but when Webb died, it was returned to him and stays in his possession, where I examined it recently. It is genuinely a horrifying object, and undeniably similar to young Wilcox's dream-sculpture.

I wasn't surprised that my uncle became fascinated by the sculptor's story, because what thoughts wouldn't arise when hearing about a sensitive young man who had dreamed not only the exact figure and hieroglyphics of the swamp-discovered image and the Greenland devil tablet, but had also encountered in his dreams at least three of the precise words from the formula spoken by both Eskimo devil-worshippers and mixed-race Louisianans—especially after learning what Legrasse had discovered about the cult? Professor Angell's immediate decision to launch the most thorough investigation possible was completely understandable; though privately I suspected that young Wilcox had somehow heard about the cult indirectly and had fabricated a series of dreams to enhance and prolong the mystery at my uncle's expense. The dream accounts and newspaper clippings that the professor had gathered were, naturally, strong supporting evidence; but my rational mindset and the outrageous nature of the entire subject led me to reach what I believed were the most reasonable conclusions. Therefore, after carefully studying the manuscript once more and comparing the theosophical and anthropological notes with Legrasse's account of the cult, I traveled to Providence to meet the sculptor and deliver the scolding I felt he deserved for so audaciously deceiving a scholarly and elderly gentleman.

Wilcox still lived by himself in the Fleur-de-Lys Building on Thomas Street, an ugly Victorian copy of seventeenth-century Breton architecture that displayed its stucco facade among the beautiful Colonial homes on the old hill, right beneath the shadow of America's most magnificent Georgian church spire. I discovered him working in his apartment, and immediately recognized from the artwork scattered around that his talent was truly deep and genuine. He will, I'm convinced, eventually be recognized as one of the great decadent artists; for he has captured in clay and will someday reflect in marble those dark dreams and visions that Arthur Machen brings to life in his writing, and Clark Ashton Smith creates in his poetry and paintings.

Dark, thin, and somewhat disheveled in appearance, he turned slowly at my knock and asked what I wanted without getting up. When I told him who I was, he showed some interest; my uncle had sparked his curiosity by investigating his strange dreams, though he had never explained why he was studying them. I didn't expand his understanding on this matter, but tried with some cleverness to get him to talk.

In a short time I became convinced of his complete honesty, because he talked about the dreams in a way that no one could misunderstand. The dreams and their unconscious effects had deeply influenced his artwork, and he showed me a disturbing sculpture whose shape nearly made me tremble with the power of its dark implications. He couldn't remember having seen the original of this object except in his own dream carving, but the form had taken shape unconsciously under his hands. It was, without question, the enormous figure he had ranted about while delirious. That he truly knew nothing about the secret cult, except for what my uncle's persistent questioning had revealed, he quickly made obvious; and once again I tried to think of some way he could possibly have received these strange impressions.

He spoke about his dreams in an unusually poetic way, making me visualize with horrifying clarity the wet, massive city built from slippery green stone—whose structure, he strangely claimed, was completely wrong—and listen with terrified anticipation to the endless, almost telepathic calling from beneath the earth: "Cthulhu fhtagn," "Cthulhu fhtagn."

These words had been part of that terrifying ritual that spoke of dead Cthulhu's dream-watch in his stone chamber at R'lyeh, and I felt deeply affected despite my logical convictions. Wilcox, I was certain, had encountered the cult in some passing manner, and had quickly forgotten it among all his other strange reading and fantasizing. Later, because of its sheer power to impress, it had emerged from his subconscious in dreams, in the carved relief, and in the horrifying statue I now looked upon; so his deception of my uncle had been completely unintentional. The young man belonged to a category that was both somewhat pretentious and somewhat rude, which I could never appreciate; but I was ready now to acknowledge both his talent and his sincerity. I said goodbye to him on friendly terms, and wished him all the success his abilities suggest he will achieve.

The subject of the cult continued to captivate me, and occasionally I imagined achieving personal recognition through investigating its origins and relationships. I traveled to New Orleans, spoke with Legrasse and other members of that historic raiding party, examined the terrifying statue, and even interviewed those mixed-race prisoners who were still alive. Old Castro, regrettably, had died several years earlier. What I learned so vividly through direct contact, while essentially just a thorough confirmation of what my uncle had documented, renewed my excitement; I was convinced that I had discovered traces of a genuine, highly secretive, and extremely ancient religion whose revelation would establish me as a distinguished anthropologist. My perspective remained one of complete materialism, as I wish it still was, and I dismissed with almost incomprehensible stubbornness the remarkable similarity between the dream records and strange newspaper clippings that Professor Angell had gathered.

One thing I started to suspect, and which I now fear I understand, is that my uncle's death was anything but natural. He fell on a narrow hillside street that led up from an old waterfront crowded with foreign sailors, after what appeared to be an accidental push from a Black seaman. I hadn't forgotten about the mixed heritage and seafaring backgrounds of the cult members in Louisiana, and it wouldn't surprise me to discover they used secret techniques and poisoned weapons as merciless and as ancient as their mysterious rituals and beliefs. Legrasse and his officers have been left alone, that much is true; but in Norway, a sailor who witnessed certain things has died. Couldn't my uncle's deeper investigations, after he encountered the sculptor's information, have reached dangerous ears? I believe Professor Angell died because he knew too much, or because he was about to learn too much. Whether I'll meet the same fate as he did remains to be seen, because I've learned a great deal myself now.

The Madness from the Sea.

If heaven ever decides to grant me a favor, it would be the complete erasure of the consequences that came from a simple accident that caused me to notice a particular piece of stray shelf-paper. It was nothing I would have naturally come across during my regular daily routine, since it was an old issue of an Australian magazine, the Sydney Bulletin from April 18, 1925. It had even escaped the attention of the clipping service that had been eagerly gathering material for my uncle's research when it was originally published.

I had mostly abandoned my research into what Professor Angell referred to as the "Cthulhu Cult," and was paying a visit to a scholarly friend in Paterson, New Jersey, who served as curator of a local museum and was a distinguished mineralogist. While examining the reserve specimens one day, which were casually arranged on storage shelves in a back room of the museum, something in one of the old newspapers spread beneath the stones caught my attention. It was the Sydney Bulletin I mentioned earlier, since my friend maintained extensive connections across all imaginable foreign regions; and the picture showed a halftone reproduction of a grotesque stone figure nearly identical to the one Legrasse had discovered in the swamp.

Eagerly emptying the page of its valuable contents, I examined the item thoroughly and was let down to discover it was only moderately long. What it implied, though, carried enormous importance for my struggling search, so I carefully ripped it out to act on it right away. It said this:

Mystery Derelict Found at Sea

Vigilant Arrives Towing Disabled Armed New Zealand Yacht. One Survivor and Dead Body Found on Board. Story of Desperate Fight and Deaths at Sea. Rescued Sailor Won't Give Details of Strange Experience. Unusual Idol Discovered in His Possession. Investigation to Follow.

The Morrison Company's cargo ship Vigilant, traveling from Valparaiso, docked this morning at its pier in Darling Harbour, towing behind it the damaged and disabled but heavily armed steam yacht Alert from Dunedin, New Zealand, which was spotted on April 12th at South Latitude 34° 21', West Longitude 152° 17', carrying one survivor and one deceased person on board.

The Vigilant departed from Valparaiso on March 25th, and by April 2nd had been pushed far south of its intended route by unusually severe storms and enormous waves. On April 12th the abandoned vessel was spotted; and although it appeared to be completely deserted, the boarding party discovered one survivor in a semi-delirious state and one man who had clearly been dead for over a week.

The living man was gripping a terrifying stone idol of mysterious origin, roughly a foot tall, whose nature has completely puzzled experts at Sydney University, the Royal Society, and the Museum in College Street, and which the survivor claims he discovered in the yacht's cabin, housed in a small carved shrine of ordinary design.

This man, after regaining consciousness, shared an incredibly bizarre tale of piracy and murder. He is Gustaf

Johansen, an intelligent Norwegian who had served as second mate aboard the two-masted schooner Emma from Auckland, which departed for Callao on February 20th with a crew of eleven men.

The Emma, he explains, was delayed and pushed far south of her intended route by the massive storm on March 1st, and on March 22nd, at South Latitude 49° 51′, West Longitude 128° 34′, came across the Alert, which was operated by a strange and menacing crew of Kanakas and mixed-race sailors. When Captain Collins was forcefully commanded to turn around, he refused; at that point, the mysterious crew started firing ruthlessly and without any warning at the schooner using an unusually powerful array of brass cannons that were part of the yacht's armament.

The crew of the Emma put up a fierce fight, according to the survivor, and even though the schooner started sinking from gunfire below the waterline, they succeeded in pulling up next to their enemy vessel and climbing aboard. They engaged in hand-to-hand combat with the brutal crew on the yacht's deck and were compelled to kill every last one of them, since the enemy slightly outnumbered them and fought in an especially vicious and desperate manner, though their fighting style was somewhat awkward.

Three crew members from the Emma, including Captain Collins and First Mate Green, lost their lives in the encounter. The surviving eight men, now under the command of Second Mate Johansen, took control of the captured yacht and continued sailing in their original direction to determine whether there had been any valid reason for the orders to turn back.

The following day, it seems, they lifted anchor and came ashore on a small island, even though no such landmass is known to exist in that region of the ocean; and six of the crew members died on land through some means, though Johansen remains strangely reluctant to discuss this portion of his account and mentions only that they fell into a rocky crevice.

Later, it appears that he and one companion got on board the yacht and attempted to handle her, but they were battered by the storm on April 2nd.

From that time until his rescue on the 12th, the man recalls very little, and he doesn't even remember when his companion William Briden died. Briden's death shows no obvious cause, and was likely the result of excitement or exposure.

Cable reports from Dunedin indicate that the Alert was well known there as an island trading vessel, and it had a bad reputation along the waterfront. The ship was owned by a strange group of mixed-race individuals whose regular meetings and nighttime journeys to the forests drew considerable attention; and it had departed in great haste immediately after the storm and earthquakes of March 1st.

Our Auckland correspondent gives the Emma and her crew an excellent reputation, and Johansen is described as a responsible and respectable man.

The admiralty will launch an investigation into the entire matter starting tomorrow, during which every attempt will be made to encourage Johansen to speak more openly than he has up to this point.

This was everything, along with the picture of that nightmarish figure; but what a flood of thoughts it unleashed in my mind! Here were fresh stores of information about the Cthulhu Cult, and proof that it had disturbing activities at sea just as much as on land. What reason drove the mixed crew to turn the Emma around as they sailed with their grotesque idol? What was that mysterious island where six of the Emma's sailors had perished, and which the mate Johansen kept so quiet about? What had the vice-admiralty's inquiry revealed, and what was known about the dangerous cult in Dunedin? And most extraordinary of all, what profound and supernatural connection of dates was this that gave a sinister and now unmistakable meaning to the different events so meticulously recorded by my uncle?

March 1st—our February 28th according to the International Date Line—the earthquake and storm had arrived. From Dunedin, the Alert and her foul crew had rushed eagerly forward as if commanded by some irresistible force, and on the opposite side of the earth, poets and artists had started to dream of a strange, damp Cyclopean city while a young sculptor had shaped in his sleep the form of the terrifying Cthulhu. March 23rd, the crew of the Emma landed on an uncharted island and left six men dead; and on that same date, the dreams of sensitive individuals took on a heightened clarity and grew dark with fear of a giant monster's evil pursuit, while an architect had lost his mind and a sculptor had suddenly fallen into madness! And what about this storm of April 2nd—the date when all dreams of the damp city stopped, and Wilcox emerged unharmed from the grip of strange fever? What about all of this—and those suggestions from old Castro regarding the sunken, star-born Old Ones and their approaching rule; their devoted cult and their control over dreams? Was I standing on the edge of cosmic terrors beyond humanity's ability to endure? If that were the case, they must be terrors of the mind alone, because somehow the second of April had ended whatever monstrous threat had begun its assault on mankind's soul.

That evening, after spending the day frantically sending telegrams and making arrangements, I said goodbye to my host and caught a train to San Francisco. Within a month, I had arrived in Dunedin, but I discovered that very little was known about the mysterious cult members who had been hanging around the old waterfront taverns. Drifters and lowlifes along the docks were too commonplace to warrant any particular attention, though there were some vague rumors about an expedition these outcasts had taken inland, during which people reported hearing faint drumbeats and seeing red flames flickering on the far-off hills.

In Auckland I discovered that Johansen had come back with his blonde hair now completely white following a brief and unsatisfactory interrogation in Sydney, and had subsequently sold his house on West Street before departing with his wife to return to his former home in Oslo. Regarding his remarkable ordeal, he refused to share any more details with his friends than he had revealed to the naval authorities, leaving them able only to provide me with his Oslo address.

After that, I traveled to Sydney and had unproductive conversations with sailors and officials from the vice-admiralty court. I spotted the Alert, which had been sold and was now being used for commercial purposes, docked at Circular Quay in Sydney Cove, but its silent presence revealed nothing useful. The crouching statue with its squid-like head, serpentine body, scaled wings, and symbol-covered base was housed in the Museum at Hyde Park; I examined it extensively and thoroughly, discovering it to be a piece of ominously beautiful craftsmanship, possessing the same complete mystery, frightening age, and otherworldly strangeness of material that I had observed in Legrasse's smaller artifact. The curator informed me that geologists had found it an incomprehensible enigma; they insisted that no rock like it existed anywhere on Earth. At that moment, I recalled with a chill what old Castro had revealed to Legrasse regarding the ancient Great Ones: "They had come from the stars, and had brought Their images with Them."

Shaken by such a profound mental upheaval as I had never experienced before, I decided to visit Mate Johansen in Oslo. I sailed to London and immediately boarded another ship bound for the Norwegian capital, arriving one autumn day at the neat docks beneath the shadow of the Egeberg.

Johansen's address, I found out, was located in the Old Town of King Harold Haardrada, which preserved the name of Oslo throughout all the centuries when the larger city disguised itself as "Christiania." I took the short journey by taxi, and knocked with a racing heart at the door of a tidy and old building with a plastered facade. A melancholy-looking woman dressed in black responded to my knock, and I felt a sharp pang of disappointment when she informed me in broken English that Gustaf Johansen was dead.

He hadn't lived long after coming back home, his wife explained, because what happened at sea in 1925 had destroyed him. He hadn't shared any more details with her than he had with the general public, but he had left behind a lengthy manuscript about "technical matters," as he called it, written in English, clearly to protect her from accidentally reading something dangerous. While walking down a narrow street near the Gothenburg dock, a stack of papers that fell from an attic window struck him and knocked him to the ground. Two Lascar sailors immediately helped him stand up, but he died before the ambulance could get to him. The doctors couldn't find a sufficient reason for his death and attributed it to heart problems and his weakened physical condition.

I could now feel that dark terror gnawing at my core, a fear that would never leave me until I too found my final rest, whether by "accident" or some other means. I convinced the widow that my involvement with her husband's "technical work" gave me enough authority to claim his manuscript, so I took the document with me and started reading it aboard the ship to London.

It was a simple, wandering piece of writing—an inexperienced sailor's attempt at creating a diary after the fact—and it tried to remember day by day that final terrible voyage. I cannot try to copy it word for word with all its confusion and repetition, but I will share enough of its main points to explain why the sound of water hitting the ship's sides became so unbearable to me that I plugged my ears with cotton.

Johansen, thank God, didn't know everything, even though he witnessed the city and the Thing, but I will never sleep peacefully again when I consider the terrors that constantly hide behind existence in time and space, and those unholy abominations from ancient stars that slumber beneath the ocean, recognized and worshipped by a nightmarish cult prepared and anxious to release them upon the world whenever another earthquake lifts their grotesque stone city back to the sunlight and open air.

Johansen's journey had started exactly as he reported it to the vice-admiralty. The Emma, carrying ballast, had departed Auckland on February 20th, and had experienced the complete fury of that earthquake-generated storm which must have thrust up from the ocean floor the terrors that haunted people's dreams. After regaining control, the vessel was making excellent headway when intercepted by the Alert on March 22nd, and I could sense the mate's sorrow as he described her bombardment and destruction. Regarding the dark-skinned cult fanatics aboard the Alert, he writes with notable revulsion. There existed some exceptionally revolting characteristic about them that made their elimination appear almost an obligation, and Johansen displays genuine bewilderment at the accusation of cruelty leveled against his group during the court of inquiry hearings. Subsequently, propelled forward by fascination in their seized yacht under Johansen's leadership, the crew spotted a massive stone column protruding from the ocean, and at S. Latitude 47° 9', W. Longitude 126° 43' discovered a shoreline of combined mud, slime, and algae-covered Cyclopean stonework which could be nothing other than the physical form of earth's ultimate horror—the nightmarish corpse-city of R'lyeh, constructed in immeasurable ages before recorded history by the enormous, repulsive entities that descended from the distant stars. There rested mighty Cthulhu and his legions, concealed in emerald viscous chambers and transmitting finally, after countless cycles, the visions that brought terror to the dreams of those susceptible and commanded urgently to the devoted to embark on a journey of freedom and renewal. None of this did Johansen realize, but heaven knows he witnessed plenty soon enough!

I believe that only a single mountaintop, the terrifying citadel crowned with monoliths where the great Cthulhu lay buried, actually rose above the water's surface. When I consider the vastness of everything that might be lurking beneath those depths, I nearly want to end my life immediately. Johansen and his crew were overwhelmed by the cosmic grandeur of this water-soaked Babylon of ancient demons, and they must have instinctively realized that it belonged neither to this world nor to any rational planet. The terror inspired by the incredible size of those greenish stone blocks, the vertigo-inducing height of the massive carved monolith, and the mind-numbing resemblance of the enormous statues and bas-reliefs to the strange idol discovered in the shrine aboard the Alert, shows clearly in every sentence of the mate's terrified account.

Without understanding what futurism was like, Johansen accomplished something remarkably similar when he described the city; rather than detailing any specific structure or building, he focused solely on the overwhelming impressions of enormous angles and stone surfaces—surfaces far too massive to belong to anything right or appropriate for this earth, and blasphemous with terrifying images and hieroglyphs. I bring up his discussion of angles because it echoes something Wilcox had shared with me about his dreadful dreams. He had explained that the geometry of the dream-place he witnessed was irregular, non-Euclidean, and disgustingly suggestive of spheres and dimensions beyond our own. Now an uneducated sailor experienced the same sensation while staring at the horrifying reality.

Johansen and his crew came ashore on a sloping muddy bank of this enormous Acropolis, and scrambled slippery up over gigantic slimy blocks that couldn't have been any human-made staircase. Even the sun in the sky appeared warped when seen through the refracting haze rising from this ocean-drenched abomination, and distorted threat and tension lurked mockingly in those wildly shifting angles of carved stone where a second look revealed hollows after the first look had shown bulges.

A feeling very much like terror had overwhelmed all the explorers before they could see anything more specific than stone and mud and seaweed. Every one of them would have run away if he hadn't been afraid of being mocked by the others, and they only searched half-heartedly—unsuccessfully, as it turned out—for some small keepsake they could take with them.

It was Rodriguez the Portuguese who climbed up the base of the monolith and called out about what he had discovered. The others followed him and stared with fascination at the enormous carved door featuring the now-recognizable squid-dragon relief sculpture. According to Johansen, it resembled a massive barn door, and they all recognized it as a door due to the elaborate lintel, threshold, and door frame surrounding it, though they couldn't determine whether it lay flat like a trapdoor or at an angle like an exterior cellar door. As Wilcox would have put it, the geometry of the place was completely wrong. No one could be certain that the sea and ground were horizontal, making the relative position of everything else seem eerily changeable.

Briden pressed against the stone in various spots, but nothing happened. Donovan then carefully examined it along the edges, testing each section individually as he moved. He made his way endlessly across the bizarre stone carving—though you could hardly call it climbing since the surface was actually horizontal—and both men marveled at how any door could possibly be so enormous. Then, very quietly and gradually, the massive panel, covering nearly an acre, started to tilt inward from the top, revealing that it was perfectly balanced.

Donovan slipped or somehow pushed himself down or along the door frame and returned to his companions, and everyone observed the strange withdrawal of the grotesquely carved doorway. In this illusion of rainbow-like distortion, it moved strangely in a slanted direction, making it seem as though all the laws of physics and visual perception had been turned upside down.

The opening was pitch black with a darkness that seemed almost solid. This blackness was truly a real force; it hid the inner walls that should have been visible, and actually erupted like smoke from its ages-long confinement, visibly dimming the sun as it crept away into the shriveled and misshapen sky on flapping skin-like wings. The smell rising from the newly opened depths was unbearable, and eventually the sharp-eared Hawkins thought he heard a disgusting, wet splashing sound down there. Everyone listened, and everyone was still listening when It stumbled droolingly into view and fumblingly forced Its jelly-like green enormity through the black doorway into the corrupted outside air of that poisoned city of madness.

Poor Johansen's handwriting nearly failed him when he wrote about this. Of the six men who never made it back to the ship, he believes two died from sheer terror in that cursed moment. The Thing cannot be described—no words exist for such depths of screaming and ancient madness, such supernatural contradictions of all matter, force, and cosmic order. A mountain walked or staggered. God! No wonder that somewhere on earth a great architect lost his mind, and poor Wilcox ranted with fever in that telepathic moment? The Thing from the idols, the green, slimy offspring of the stars, had awakened to reclaim what was his. The stars had aligned once more, and what an ancient cult had failed to accomplish through planning, a group of innocent sailors had achieved by chance. After countless eons great Cthulhu was free again, and hungry for destruction.

Three men were caught by the flabby claws before anyone could react. May God grant them peace, if any peace exists in the universe. Those men were Donovan, Guerrera and Angstrom. Parker stumbled as the other three frantically scrambled across endless stretches of green-encrusted rock toward the boat, and Johansen swears Parker was consumed by a corner of stonework that had no business being there; a corner that appeared sharp but acted as though it were rounded. So only Briden and Johansen made it to the boat, rowing desperately toward the Alert as the enormous monstrosity tumbled down the slippery stones and paused, struggling at the water's edge.

Steam hadn't been allowed to die down completely, even though all the crew had left for the shore; and it took only a few frantic moments of rushing back and forth between the wheels and engines to get the Alert moving. Slowly, surrounded by the twisted horrors of that impossible scene, the ship began to churn through the deadly waters; while on the stone shore of that death-filled coast that wasn't of this earth, the massive Thing from the stars drooled and babbled like Polyphemus cursing Odysseus's escaping ship. Then, more daring than the legendary Cyclops, great Cthulhu slipped greasily into the water and started chasing them with enormous wave-creating strokes of cosmic power. Briden looked back and lost his mind, laughing wildly as he continued laughing on and off until death took him one night in the cabin while Johansen wandered in delirium.

But Johansen hadn't given up yet. He knew the Thing could easily catch up to the Alert before the steam engine reached full power, so he decided on a desperate gamble. Setting the engine to maximum speed, he rushed up to the deck like lightning and spun the wheel around. The foul seawater churned and foamed violently, and as the steam pressure built higher and higher, the courageous Norwegian aimed his ship directly at the pursuing mass of jelly that loomed above the dirty foam like the back end of a demonic warship. The terrifying squid head with its twisting tentacles came almost close enough to touch the front of the sturdy yacht, but Johansen pressed forward without mercy.

There was an explosion like a bursting balloon, a wet and disgusting mess like a split fish, a smell like a thousand open graves, and a sound that the writer refused to describe on paper. For a moment the ship was covered by a sharp and blinding green cloud, and then there was only a poisonous bubbling behind them; where—dear God!—the scattered remains of that unnameable creature from the sky were mysteriously coming back together in its horrible original shape, while it grew more distant every second as the Alert picked up speed from its increasing steam power.

That was all. After that, Johansen could only brood over the idol in the cabin and take care of a few basic food needs for himself and the laughing madman beside him. He didn't attempt to steer the ship after that first daring escape, because the shock had drained something from his very soul. Then the storm hit on April 2nd, and darkness began closing in around his mind. There's a feeling of ghostly spinning through endless liquid voids, of nauseating rides through tilting universes while clinging to a comet's tail, and of frenzied plunges from the depths to the moon and from the moon back down to the depths again, all accompanied by the cackling laughter of the twisted, gleeful ancient gods and the green, bat-winged jeering demons of hell.

Out of that dream came salvation—the Vigilant, the vice-admiralty court, the streets of Dunedin, and the lengthy journey back home to the old house by the Egeberg. He couldn't tell anyone—they would consider him insane. He would write about what he understood before death arrived, but his wife must not suspect. Death would be a blessing if only it could erase the memories.

That was the document I read, and I've now placed it in the metal box next to the carved relief and Professor Angell's papers. Along with it will go this account of mine—this examination of my own mental state, where I've assembled what I hope will never be put together again. I have witnessed everything the universe contains of terror, and even spring skies and summer flowers will forever be tainted for me. But I don't believe my life will last much longer. Just as my uncle died, just as poor Johansen died, so will I. I know far too much, and the cult continues to exist.

Cthulhu still lives, I believe, once again in that stone chasm that has protected him since the sun was young. His cursed city has sunk beneath the waves once more, for the Vigilant sailed over that very location after the April storm; but his servants on earth continue to roar and dance and kill around idol-crowned monoliths in remote places. He must have been caught by the sinking while trapped within his dark abyss, or else the world would already be filled with screams of terror and madness. Who can know how this will end? What has emerged may sink again, and what has sunk may rise once more. Horror waits and dreams in the depths, and corruption spreads across the crumbling cities of humanity. A time will come—but I must not and cannot allow myself to think about it! Let me hope that, if I do not survive this manuscript, those who handle my affairs will choose caution over boldness and ensure that no other eyes ever see it.

THE END

Thank You For Reading

You've Just Read a Piece of the Greatest Library Ever Rebuilt

Thank you for reading.

This book is one of thousands we're restoring, reimagining, and translating as part of the **Modern Library of Alexandria** — a global movement to preserve and share humanity's most important ideas.

What was once lost to fire and time is now rising again — not just as memory, but as living, breathing knowledge, freely accessible to all.

What You Can Do Next:

- **Keep Reading.**

  Discover more legendary works — in beautiful print, audiobook, or digital form — at LibraryofAlexandria.com.

- **Build Your Own Library.**

  Every title is available as a paperback, hardcover, or collectible boxset — at true printing cost. Craft a personal library worthy of display.

- **Spread the Light.**

  Share this book. Tell others about the movement. Help us translate every timeless work into every language, so no reader is ever left behind.

By finishing this book, you've already taken part in something extraordinary.

Join us at LibraryofAlexandria.com

Together, we're rebuilding the greatest library the world has ever known.

With appreciation,

The Modern Library of Alexandria Team

Visit:
www.libraryofalexandria.com
Or scan the code below:

www.ingramcontent.com/pod-product-compliance
Lightning Source LLC
Chambersburg PA
CBHW010139030826
48979CB00023B/1034

* 9 7 8 1 8 0 6 2 9 9 4 7 8 *